The TRANSFORMERS™— Robots in Disguise!

They came from Cybertron—a planet of machines—where war raged for thousands of years between the noble Autobots and the evil Decepticons.

NOW THE BATTLE OF THESE POWERFUL ROBOTS IS YOUR BATTLE!

ONLY YOU can protect the earth from the evil destruction of the Decepticons!

Read the directions at the bottom of each page. Then decide what the Autobots should do next.

If you decide correctly, the Autobots will triumph! If you make the wrong choices, the unspeakable evil of the Decepticons will rule the world!

Hurry! The adventure begins on page 1.

THE TRANSFORMERS™

Autobot Alert!

by Judith Bauer Stamper

BALLANTINE BOOKS • NEW YORK

Library of Congress Catalog Card Number: 86-90732

ISBN: 0-345-33388-8

Editorial Services by Parachute Press, Inc.

Illustrated by William Schmidt

Designed by Gene Siegel

Manufactured in the United States of America

First Edition: September 1986

10 9 8 7 6 5 4 3 2 1

THE TRANSFORMERS™

Autobot Alert!

Inside the Autobot city, Metroplex, Hot Rod jogs back from his karate lessons. The teenage Autobot grabs an energon cube from a production line he passes.

"Seems like I'm always starving," he mutters, popping the high-energy treat into his mouth. Then he sees his old pal, Kup, ahead of him.

"Hey, Kup!" Hot Rod yells, "what's been going on? I know you've got some big secret!"

Kup turns around with a creak. He sizes up the sleek, new-model Autobot who is like a grandson to him.

"What secret?" the old veteran snorts.

"Come on, Kup, give me a hint," Hot Rod begs. "I know Beachcomber, Springer, and Blurr left on a special mission two days ago."

"How did you find that out!" Kup asks in amazement.

. . . .

Turn to page 8 to find out more.

You decide the Autobots should raise the ship themselves. Blurr makes some quick calculations. The Decepticons should be flying above Tucson, Arizona, at this very moment. The Autobots have exactly 28 minutes and 14 seconds to find the cybertite sphere and make a getaway!

"Every second counts!" Ultra Magnus tells the Autobots. The Autobot leader looks over his band of warriors. He must devise a strategy that combines strength, speed, and intelligence. His Autobots stand at attention, each ready to sacrifice himself to save the ancient secret.

One minute passes—then two—then three. Ultra Magnus has come up with three possible plans.

The first strategy relies mainly on the powerful Dinobot Sludge. Ultra Magnus has singled him out because of his immense strength and ability to work in water. The Dinobot's mission will be to circle the ship with cables, raise it from the ocean bottom, and bring it back to land where Hot Rod can search for the cybertite. Sludge's power is undeniable. The question is, will he work fast enough?

To hear about your other two choices, go on to page 3.

The second strategy uses the energetic and seaworthy Autobot Seaspray. His mission will be to search the *Seville* underwater and bring back the cybertite sphere. The plan sounds logical . . . but it relies totally on the performance of one rather small Autobot!

The third strategy is based on the teamwork of Grapple, Bumblebee, and Hot Rod. Bumblebee will hook Grapple's crane to the *Seville*. Hot Rod will search for the cybertite sphere. Grapple will be in charge of lifting the ship. Teamwork works . . . most of the time.

The Decepticons are coming closer by the second. You must pick a course of action!

. . . .

If you want Sludge to raise the ship, turn to page 5.

If you want Seaspray to search the ship underwater, turn to page 62.

If you think it's wisest to trust this to the teamwork of Grapple, Bumblebee, and Hot Rod, turn to page 67.

"Prepare battle stations," orders Ultra Magnus, "for an all-out attack on Cyclonus!"

"But . . . that could be suicide!" Mirage says.

"We have no choice," insists Ultra Magnus. "Let's just hope Galvatron isn't on board to help Cyclonus fight back."

As the Autobots hurry to their battle stations Powerglide pulls Swoop aside. "I don't like this," Powerglide whispers. "The only way to beat a Decepticon is by playing his own game—deception!"

Powerglide draws Swoop into a huddle and plans a strategy of his own to battle Cyclonus. Meanwhile, Ultra Magnus positions the shuttle's weapons on the distant air warrior. This is a difficult moment for the Autobots. Their commander has formulated a strategy that comes from his years of experience. Yet some of his warriors doubt his wisdom.

Powerglide is confident about his surprise attack, but he's a known show-off.

Put yourself in command of the space shuttle. Whose strategy will you choose to destroy the evil Cyclonus?

. . . .

For Ultra's Magnus's all-out attack, turn to page 24.

To send Powerglide and Swoop into action, turn to page 46.

4

"Sludge," Ultra Magnus commands, "step forward."

A look of amazement slowly spreads over the shy Dinobot's face.

"Who? Me?" he asks the Autobot leader.

"Sludge! Step forward!" Ultra Magnus repeats impatiently. He is beginning to wonder about this decision!

The Dinobot takes one giant step forward, causing an earth tremor on the cliff.

Ultra Magnus steadies his footing and then explains the Dinobot's mission.

"Me do it!" Sludge exclaims. "Wade into water . . . lift up ship . . . bring back to beach."

"Good, Sludge, very good," Ultra Magnus says as Hot Rod gives the Dinobot the cable. "Now *hurry up and do it!*"

The Dinobot slides down the cliff into the water, making a small avalanche of rocks. Then he does his dinosaur version of a dog paddle out to the sunken ship.

"Now what?" he calls back to Ultra Magnus, and the cable falls from his mouth and sinks into the water.

Ultra Magnus wears a pained look. Was this a good idea?

. . . .

Turn to page 71.

Kup continues his story. "Last month Beach-comber, our Autobot geologist, discovered fragments of cybertite. They were embedded in a meteor crater in the southwest desert. I sent Blurr and Springer to help him search for the ancient formula.

"What have they found? We do not know—for the answer is in the hands of the Decepticons!"

A chorus of angry voices swells through the Autobot city.

"Hurryuphurryuphurryuphurryuphurryup . . . .Backtothedesertbacktothedesert, . . ." Blurr reels off.

Ultra Magnus raises his hand for silence.

"Our mission is to find the ancient formula. Our goal is to triumph over the Decepticons. Autobots, start your engines . . . and . . . *transform!*"

Metroplex vibrates with the roar of racing engines. Blurr streaks out in the lead. The other Autobots speed after him.

What will they discover in the far-off desert? To find out . . .

. . . .

Turn to page 16.

"I saw them leave," Hot Rod answers Kup with a sly smile, "while I was out for a midnight spin."

"Listen, kid," the old veteran insists, "this mission is top priority. That's why Ultra Magnus put me in charge!"

"What do *you* know about the new Autobot systems?" Hot Rod asks, trying to bait his friend.

"Who said it's about new-fangled systems? It's about the old days," Kup barks back. "The old days on Cybertron!" But before he can explain further, Ultra Magnus strides up.

Hot Rod salutes. "Hello, sir," he says respectfully. The Autobot leader salutes him in return.

Kup is about to speak when suddenly an alarm sounds throughout the Autobot city. The robots stare up at the computer monitor hanging from the ceiling. Red letters flash on the screens: AUTOBOT ALERT! AUTOBOT ALERT!

Next a picture of Cosmos, the Autobot communications satellite, appears.

"Quiet!" Ultra Magnus orders. "An important message from Earth orbit!"

. . . .

Turn to page 11.

The shark bares a row of razor-sharp teeth. A shark may not be able to do much harm to a robot, but Seaspray can't risk losing the sphere in a struggle. He reaches for his underwater laser gun. The shark attacks! Seaspray stuns it with a laser blast at a range of two feet!

The robot clutches the cybertite sphere and propels himself up to the surface of the water. The Autobots cheer as their friend emerges, holding the ancient secret.

Seaspray speeds back to land and delivers his prize into the hands of his leader.

It's no secret now . . . you chose a good ending. The Autobots carry the sphere safely back to headquarters before the enemy even arrives.

Soon, the Decepticons will go fishing for the cybertite sphere, but all they'll find is a ghostly ship and a very irritated shark.

THE END

"Fall back into your ambush positions," the Autobot commander orders. "Toss that sphere to Blurr, Hot Rod," he adds.

The precious sphere soars through the air. Every Autobot holds his breath. Blurr positions himself underneath it like an outfielder. It falls into his hands in a perfect catch. Immediately, the lightning-fast messenger transforms and is off in a streak heading for Metroplex.

Seconds later the first wave of Decepticon planes roars over the cliff to search the waters for the *Seville*.

"Fire!" Ultra Magnus commands.

One by one, the Autobots pick off the enemy jets from the sky. The Decepticons plummet into the choppy waters below, sputtering oaths and spewing out fish.

It's too late for the second wave of Decepticons to reverse their engines. They fly over the Autobots, exposing their undersides to the ambush attack.

Plop! Splash! Plop! Crash!

The Decepticons go down in defeat, to a sleep in the deep!

THE END

Cosmos's mechanical voice beeps from the monitor. "Red alert situation! Red alert situation! Decepticon activity in nearby space. Very suspicious. Enemy sighted to the right! Enemy approaching rapidly! . . . Red Alert situa—"

The voice of Cosmos drowns in sharp static. Seconds later his image disappears!

"He's been zapped!" Hot Rod shouts.

A murmur of worried voices builds in the room. Then Bumblebee rushes in.

"Really weird!" he exclaims. "I was watching a baseball game on TV and all of a sudden the picture fuzzed out. Then the Decepticon symbol started flashing on!"

"This is what Cosmos was trying to warn us about," Hot Rod declares.

"Just what I suspected!" Ultra Magnus booms out. "The Decepticons are behind this! They've taken over Earth's communications satellites! And they've sabotaged Cosmos!"

"Uh-oh," Kup mutters, pointing down a long hallway. "I think more bad news is on the way!"

Turn to page 26.

11

"What good will the ancient secret do us," Ultra Magnus demands, "if we are all Decepticon slaves? Their power in space must be destroyed!"

The Autobot leader strides into the central computer room in the headquarters.

"Bumblebee," he orders, "bring me your TV set . . . on the double!"

The others crowd around Ultra Magnus while he uses the computers to search for Cosmos's last coordinates in space.

"We must rescue our fallen friend," the Autobot commander reminds everyone. Ultra Magnus is famous for his loyalty to the Autobots.

"Look, it's Galvatron!" Bumblebee shouts as he bursts into the room with his portable TV.

The Autobots gaze in horror at the screen. Galvatron stares back. The Decepticon leader booms out a dire message to the people of Earth.

"I am Galvatron, the new master of your planet," he announces. "You have nothing to fear . . . as long as you follow my commands. Stay tuned, and don't bother to turn your dial—I'm on all the channels!"

Turn to page 25.

"We have chosen the path of strength through cunning," Ultra Magnus says. "Now we must conceal ourselves in these cliffs and wait for the Decepticons."

The Autobots climb down the steep, jagged rocks that are dotted with caves and crevices. One by one, the robots disappear from sight. The cliffs appear to be deserted except for a few roosting seagulls.

Then, suddenly, the gulls screech and rise into the air, panic-stricken. From their hiding places, the Autobots hear the approaching roar of Decepticon engines. Soon the air is filled with the deafening sound of Decepticon landing gear hitting the cliffs. The very rock trembles beneath their weight.

The enemy leader—the evil and arrogant Galvatron—transforms into his robot shape on the highest pinnacle of the cliffs.

"Total power is within our reach!" he announces to his followers. "Raise the ship and find the Autobot secret . . . and we will know strength beyond our wildest dreams!"

This Decepticon dream may turn out to be a nightmare for the Autobots!

Turn to page 54.

"The Constructicons have been working over-time," Hot Rod mutters. He points to a complex of new buildings around Astrotrain.

"The control center for the Decepticon space plot!" says Bumblebee. "This must be where the jamming device is located!"

The two Autobots study the layout of the enemy complex. Then Hot Rod hoists the backpack of laser weapons onto his shoulders. He gestures to Bumblebee.

"Let's go," he says, taking charge. "I'll check out their security system."

"I've already checked it out," Bumblebee snaps back. "Remember, I have the best vision of all the Autobots. And I was in the spy business before you even had your circuits wired!"

Hot Rod's fuel lines warm with embarrassment. For a minute there, he had forgotten that Bumblebee was his senior.

"We'll sneak inside right there," Bumblebee continues. He points to a corridor of trees left standing between two sections of the control center.

"And remember," he adds with a stern look, "don't try to be a hotshot, Hot Rod!"

Turn to page 23.

14

The caravan of Autobots screeches to a halt at the desert research center. For a moment they just stare at the wrecked building, riddled by Decepticon bullets.

"Hurry, Ratchet. Inside," Ultra Magnus orders. "Get Springer back in shape again."

The Autobot mechanic searches all over the building for his friend's parts. It's like putting together a jigsaw puzzle. But at last the unsprung Springer bounces back to life.

"The message!" he exclaims. "Did you get it, Kup?"

"The Decepticons got it," Kup answers. "Tell me what it said!"

"The cybertite sphere wasn't in the meteor," Springer explains. "Someone beat us to it—a long time ago."

"Who?" Ultra Magnus demands.

"People who had no idea what they had found," Springer says. "They were sixteenth-century Spanish explorers from the ship *Seville*. We found a diary belonging to one of the sailors. It said the sphere was being carried back to Spain!"

"Adios!" Hot Rod says. "I'm on my way!"

"Wait!" says Springer.

Turn to page 57.

Hot Rod punches a sequence of buttons on the keyboard. Scourge grabs his arms in a hammerlock. But the Decepticon is too late!

Every set of eyes in the room focuses on the huge monitor as a shower of missiles spurts out from Astrotrain. Red arrows trace their paths across space . . . straight into the air warrior Cyclonus! The Autobot space shuttle stops in its trajectory. Then it zooms away to safety!

For Hot Rod and Bumblebee, victory is sweet but short. Scourge savagely picks them up and throws them across his shoulders. The evil Decepticon chortles as he walks toward the big door of Astrotrain. He giggles hideously as he swings it open. He laughs demoniacally as he throws the two Autobots out into the vast blackness of space.

All is silent. The Autobots drift helplessly through the vacuum around them. . . . waiting . . . waiting . . . for the rescue that may never come!

THE END

The Autobot leader and his team don their special space gear for solar protection. Then they enter
the shuttle.

With a fiery burst of orange flames, the space
shuttle roars into the clear blue sky over the Pacific
Northwest. Soon the shuttle enters the outer at-
mosphere and then Earth's orbit.

The shuttle hurtles on through space toward
Cosmos's last coordinates.

"Cut the engines, Jazz!" Ultra Magnus suddenly
orders.

The vehicle hovers to a stop in orbit. Looking out
a side window Powerglide points and yells, "There's
Cosmos!"

But from the front window of the command post,
Ultra Magnus has sighted something else.

"We have company," he murmurs gravely. "Galvatron's spaceship."

The Autobots follow their leader's gaze as far as
they can see. There, in the distance, sits the evil, the
powerful, the destructive Decepticon space warrior—
Cyclonus.

Turn to page 59.

The teenage Autobot turns away from the window. He stares at Astrotrain's military command post. If only he could get his hands on the controls for just a few seconds! Then the Autobot shuttle could be warned. Hot Rod knows his chances of getting through the guards aren't very good. But the reward would be worth the risk!

The young robot feels the weight of the laser weapons on his back. They are his other choice. If he could find a good hiding place, he could shoot them at Cyclonus. The Autobots would hear the explosion . . . and see the danger ahead of them. *If* the plan worked.

Hot Rod needs your help. The fate of the Autobots is in his hands . . . and yours. Decide now . . . and prepare for the consequences.

If you want Hot Rod to commandeer the military controls of Astrotrain, turn to page 68.

If you want him to find a hiding place from which he can fire at Cyclonus, turn to page 33.

19

At the control deck the Autobot leader inspects a computer graphic. It is being drawn by high-powered sensors that are focused on the distant Cyclonus.

The Autobots study the graphic carefully. They detect a complex grid of transmitters attached to Cyclonus's metal skin. The transmitters are beaming incredibly strong electrical signals down to Earth.

"That's it!" Mirage exclaims. "Cyclonus is the giant jamming device!"

"We'd better think fast," Ultra Magnus mutters, "before he jams us!"

Turn to page 4.

The silence among the Autobots is suddenly broken as arguments over strategy break out. Kup and Blurr insist that the secret mission has top priority. An ancient formula is at stake. It could change the balance of power between the Autobots and the Decepticons forever!

Ultra Magnus and Bumblebee argue that the space plot is an even greater threat to the balance of power. If the Decepticons can control Earth's military satellites, they can destroy the freedom of the planet's inhabitants forever!

The Autobots can't decide. You must remain calm and take over. Consider your options. Weigh the arguments. Then decide! Will you choose an offensive against the Decepticons in space? Or will you choose to rescue the ancient Autobot secret?

To take on the Decepticons in space, turn to page 12.
To go for the ancient secret, turn to page 35.

The two Autobots descend into the valley of the Decepticons. Hot Rod gulps—he's just begun to realize how dangerous this plan is. The entire complex hums like a war machine!

The Autobots dodge from tree to tree through the wooded corridor and into the heart of the enemy's stronghold. Bumblebee's keen eyes dart back and forth, on the lookout for guards. At last they reach the end of their forest cover. Before them lies an open area stripped of vegetation.

"Astrotrain's launch site!" Hot Rod exclaims.

"Sh-sh-sh!" Bumblebee hisses, pointing to the left.

Frenzy and Ravage walk by, discussing Decepticon strategy. The two Autobots flatten themselves behind a large redwood.

"Takeoff time is in ten minutes," Ravage mutters.

"The beginning of the end for the Autobots!" Frenzy adds with a leer.

Turn to page 34.

Ultra Magnus stands on the observation deck, staring at Cyclonus. His iron fists are clenched so tightly that they throw off friction sparks.

"Prowl," he orders, "program the engines for fast-forward thrust. Jazz, commence firing the laser cannons when we reach a range of fifty kilometers."

The Autobots on board nervously prepare for the attack. The shuttle is filled with a feeling of dread. Suddenly the spaceship shoots forward toward its moment of reckoning with the giant Decepticon.

Cyclonus looms larger and larger as they approach him.

"Now!" Ultra Magnus commands. "Fire!"

A burst of laser power rips a hole into the side of the air warrior. A sickening, mechanical roar booms out through the universe. Then Cyclonus spins about and sights his attacker.

"Fools!" roars a voice from inside Cyclonus. As the Autobots watch in horror Galvatron emerges from Cyclonus! And an army of Decepticons behind him transforms into devastating multiwing jet fighters!

Turn to page 32.

As Galvatron's image fades, the Autobot commander puts in a call to Ratchet in the garage of Metroplex.

"Ratchet, prepare the space shuttle for takeoff. And double-check the weaponry systems. We must have total firepower!"

The Autobots eagerly crowd around Ultra Magnus. They all know what he will say next.

"I'll need five good Autobots to come with me," the leader announces. His eyes sweep across the robots crowded around him. "Jazz . . . Mirage . . . Swoop . . . Powerglide . . . and Prowl. Prepare for takeoff!"

A loud buzz erupts from the intercom in the control room. Then the voice of Ratchet, the Autobot medical officer, bursts into the room.

"Big trouble, chief," he reports. "There's a malfunction in the shuttle's engine."

"Get on it right away," Ultra Magnus commands. "We'll stand by."

Standing by, in a corner of the room, is Hot Rod. The teenage Autobot has a scowl on his face. Disappointment and jealousy gleam in his eyes.

Turn to page 58.

The other Autobots follow Kup's gaze to a streak of movement hurtling toward them. The image comes to a sudden stop. Then it materializes into the lightning-fast Autobot messenger, Blurr. In a split second Blurr reels off a garbled message at a million words per minute. He sounds like a tape recorder gone berserk!

"Blurr!" Ultra Magnus shouts. "You're going to break the sound barrier. Slow down so we can understand you."

"Kup,it'saboutyoursecretmissioninthedesert—" Blurr begins.

"Slower!" Ultra Magnus insists, grabbing the robot's jaw.

"Kup, it's about your secret mission in the desert!" Blurr repeats. "Decepticon storm troopers blasted into our research center. They short-circuited Springer. They dragged Beachcomber away. And the worst is . . . they stole a top secret, coded message Springer wrote. It was for your eyes only, Kup!"

"Decepticon eyes must not read it!" Kup moans. "The ancient Autobot secret cannot fall into their hands! We must rescue it—right now!"

. . . .

Go on to page 27.

"But what about the Decepticons in space?" Bumblebee demands. "They're jamming satellite transmissions. Soon they'll control all of the communications on Earth."

"That means all of the information that Earthlings receive will come from the Decepticons," says Hot Rod. "It's the first step toward total control of the planet!"

The Autobots stand in stunned silence. The Decepticons have attacked on two fronts, and it's hard to tell which attack is a greater threat.

Turn to page 22.

The Autobots follow Hound's lead to a craggy, deserted area of the California coast. They line up on the high cliffs above the crashing waves of the Pacific Ocean. Out over the water, Powerglide's search finally comes to an end. Grinning, he circles a spot above the choppy water. This is where the Spanish galleon, the *Seville*, sank, with the cybertite sphere in its hold.

"Transform!" Ultra Magnus orders. The Autobot vehicles become mighty robots standing on the cliffs. They crowd around their leader, waiting to hear his plans for raising the ship. Just as Ultra Magnus is about to speak, Blurr streaks onto the scene.

"They'rehalfwayherethey'rehalfwayherethey're-halfwayhere . . . theDecepticonsknowabouttheformula . . . actfastactfastactfastactfastactfast!"

Don't just sit there! Turn to page 31!

"Ready to spring a surprise on the Decepticons?" Springer asks Topspin and Seaspray.

"Aye-aye, Captain," Seaspray says with a salute.

"All right then," Springer continues. "You two sneak down to the coast about a mile away. When I see you coming back on the water, I'll make my move."

The two oceangoing Autobots steal across the cliffs in robot mode. Springer follows a little way and then conceals himself under a ledge jutting out just over the beached ship. Seaspray and Topspin continue down toward the shore.

It's a tense wait for Springer. The Decepticons have begun to climb aboard the *Seville*. Springer wonders if they'll beat the Autobots to the cybertite sphere.

Moments later a battle cry rings out from the Decepticon lookouts on the cliff. They point out into the water. Every Decepticon's eyes follow.

It's Seaspray and Topspin! They're speeding through the ocean in their vessel modes. They are heading straight for the Constructicons, their lasers blasting away.

Springer poises on the edge of the cliff as the Decepticons scramble out of the *Seville*.

Now, Springer. *Jump!*

Turn to page 42.

By now, Ultra Magnus can decode Blurr's speeded-up speech. He knows a quick decision must be made.

The Autobot commander gathers his best advisers about him. They discuss two possible strategies.

One: The Autobots can raise the ship, find the cybertite sphere, and try to get away before the Decepticons arrive. It's a good idea—if there's enough time to make it work!

Two: The Autobots can conceal themselves, let the Decepticons do the dirty work of bringing up the ship, and then steal the cybertite sphere in an ambush attack.

Ultra Magnus just pointed his finger at you. It's your decision. And you have less than five seconds to make it!

To raise the ship, turn to page 2.
To hide and ambush the Decepticons, turn to page 13.

Ultra Magnus gulps. How can he counter Galvatron's jets? A scream from Mirage interrupts his thoughts.

"Retreat!" Mirage yells in a choked voice. Then he crumples into a heap as a blast from Galvatron's laser gun hits the side of the shuttle.

The Autobot leader rushes to the ship's computer. He punches in a reverse-engine command. The shuttle shudders to a stop, throwing the Autobots across the room. But before the ship can change course, a bomb with the punch of a meteor hits it.

"The shuttle is splitting!" Swoop cries out. The Autobots watch helplessly as their ship breaks apart.

The roar of Decepticon laughter is heard throughout the galaxy. Galvatron and Cyclonus grin triumphantly as pieces of the Autobot space shuttle drift through space.

And for the Earthlings, the future is bleak. The Decepticons will be their masters . . . and television programs will be worse than ever!

THE END

"We've got to find a hiding place all right," Bumblebee whispers. "Here comes Laserbeak!"

The cruel Decepticon interrogator is striding down the corridor toward them.

"Just seeing him gives me a headache," the mini-car groans. Bumblebee has fought Laserbeak before and he's a fierce enemy.

Hot Rod spots a nearby door. Its sign reads DIRTY TRICKS DEPARTMENT. He pulls Bumblebee inside just as Laserbeak sights them in the corridor.

"Whew! We're alone," Hot Rod murmurs as he looks around the small room.

"Listen," the mini-car whispers. "He's coming closer!"

The two Autobots hear the heavy footsteps of Laserbeak approaching.

"He's going to come in here," says Bumblebee. "This is his department, you know . . . dirty tricks!"

Turn to page 40.

"Did you hear that?" whispers Hot Rod. "We've got to get aboard Astrotrain before launch time!"

"Too risky," says Bumblebee. "I want to infiltrate the control center."

The two Autobots stare at each other, locked in a battle of iron wills. This is no time for an argument! Looks like you'll have to take control of the mission.

Hot Rod wants to stow away on Astrotrain. On board, the Autobots could stop the Decepticons' dirty deeds. Then again, they could get caught—and dropped onto a planet full of monsters who like Autobot appetizers.

Bumblebee thinks the control center on Earth is the best target. The whole operation is being run from there. The two Autobots could blow it up . . . if they can beat the Decepticons to the punch.

There's no more time to sit around and think. The countdown has begun on the Decepticon space shuttle.

To send Hot Rod and Bumblebee onto Astrotrain, turn to page 36.

To keep them on the ground, turn to page 64.

Of all the Autobots, Blurr seems most anxious to retrieve the stolen coded message. "Hurryhurry-hurryhurryhurryhurryhurry . . ." he repeats, tapping his foot so fast that it becomes a white streak.

Ultra Magnus, Ratchet, Kup, Hot Rod, and a battle force of other Autobots prepare for the journey to the desert research center. The Autobot leader takes Kup aside to confer with him. Then he demands the attention of everyone at headquarters.

"There is an ancient Autobot secret," he announces. "None of you know what it is. But you will be risking your lives to save it. Listen while our old comrade Kup tells you a story from the days on Cybertron."

The grizzled Autobot veteran summons all of his dignity and steps forward. He loves to tell a story, and now all the Autobots stand before him—a captive audience.

"It is a secret of strength," Kup begins, "a secret of power!"

Not a sound breaks the silence. The ancient secret is about to be revealed!

Turn to page 61.

A Constructicon rumbles by, pulling a trailer full of bombs for Astrotrain. Hot Rod grabs Bumblebee and hoists him up for a ride on the trailer. The two Autobots crouch down under the huge rockets built to destroy them.

"I hope we don't hit a big bump," says Bumblebee nervously.

"Yeah," Hot Rod agrees. "This could turn into a dynamite ride!"

The Constructicon unhitches the trailer inside the munitions hold of Astrotrain. The two Autobots remain in their hiding places until they feel the huge spaceship lift off the ground.

"Look!" Hot Rod whispers to Bumblebee as four Decepticons come out of a door marked SPACE GEAR. They are dressed in silver suits and gas masks cover their faces.

"A perfect disguise for us!" the mini-car murmurs. "I just hope those suits come in size eight short."

"Come on," urges Hot Rod, "the coast is clear."

Will the Autobots be able to get in gear? To find out . . .

. . . .

Turn to page 50.

36

"California, here we come!" Hot Rod yells, eager to head for the coast.

"Silence, Autobots!" Ultra Magnus commands. "Our mission must succeed. And each of us must do his special part."

The Autobot leader gives out assignments to his robots, one by one. Powerglide must fly ahead and search the waters off the coast for the sunken ship. Blurr must go to the meteor crater and find out what the Decepticons know—and what they did with Beachcomber. Hound must scout ahead for the best route to the coast. The rest of the Autobots are assigned important jobs matched to their special skills.

"Never forget," says Ultra Magnus at the end, "we desperately need the ancient formula. Once it is in our hands, we must protect it at all costs . . . and take it back to Metroplex!"

At a signal from their leader, the Autobots rev their engines, get in gear, and zoom west to the Pacific.

To catch up with them, turn to page 28.

Hot Rod hears a familiar drone in the air. He looks to the east. A formation of Decepticon fighter planes is headed straight toward them.

"Autobot alert!" the teenage robot screams.

But the enemy is too quick. Before the Autobots can set up a defense, the planes are on top of them. Galvatron is in the lead, spewing out bombs and missiles. Ramjet, Blitzwing, Dirge, Thrust, and Frenzy pulverize the *Seville* dangling from Grapple's hook. Bumblebee jumps into the sea seconds before the ship—and the cybertite sphere—are blown to smithereens!

The ancient formula is lost forever! The Autobots are being pounded by enemy firepower. This is a bad news ending with only one cliffhanger. . . .

That's Hot Rod. He jumped off Grapple's hook when the Decepticons started their attack. But he missed his landing spot by a few inches. Now he's hanging off the edge of the cliff . . . by the tips of his iron fingernails!

THE END

Laserbeak's footsteps pause outside the door. Inside, the Autobots freeze as they hear Frenzy's voice scream down the hallway.

"Laserbeak, get your ugly beak to the control room—on the double!"

Bumblebee heaves a sigh of relief as his enemy hurries away.

Meanwhile, Hot Rod checks out the room. He finds a hatch to the outside of the space shuttle. Very carefully, the teenage Autobot opens his case of laser weapons. He pulls out a rapid-fire, high-intensity rifle cannon.

"Plug your ears, Bumblebee," he warns. "Perceptor said this could blow away a skyscraper at a close range. Let's see what it does to Cyclonus."

Hot Rod squints into the sights of the weapon, training it on the distant air warrior. He pulls the trigger.

Boom!

For a second the universe seems to explode!

Pick yourself up off the floor and turn to page 48.

Urged on by Brawn and Ironhide, Grapple spins out his grappling hook to the ship on the beach below. It latches on like an iron fist. Then the Autobot reels the galleon up like a huge, hooked fish.

"Stop them!" the furious voice of Galvatron screams out, echoing for miles up and down the coast.

Decepticon laser blasters, machine guns, disintegrator beams, and heavy artillery cannons are unleashed. Frenzy, Dirge, Ramjet, and Thrust take off into the air from the cliffs. Out over the water, they spin around and attack Grapple full force!

From the caves, Brawn, Ironhide, and the other Autobots try to defend the ship. But the *Seville* is caught in the laser cross fire. It explodes into a million pieces that fall like rain into the sea.

"It's gone—forever!" Kup cries out. "The ancient Autobot secret is destroyed!"

The Decepticons continue their furious attack on the cliffs! The Autobots are trapped in their caves! Could they ever use a power booster now!

Moral: Never use Brawn without brains.

THE END

As the Decepticon fighters take off from the top of the cliffs, Springer leaps off the ledge, his powerful muscles springing him into the air like a pogo stick. Down, down, down, he falls—right into the hold of the *Seville*! Right away, he goes to work searching for the cybertite sphere.

Meanwhile, Seaspray and Topspin are churning up the ocean, escaping from Decepticon firepower. Topspin guns his two rear jet engines and streaks over the waves at three hundred miles per hour! Seaspray outmaneuvers the Decepticon planes above him, right at home in naval battle.

Back in the ship's hold, Springer opens an old leather chest. Inside lies a glowing green ball—the cybertite sphere! The ancient Autobot secret is in safe hands at last!

But will it be safe for long?

Turn to page 72.

"Forget the code!" Hot Rod insists. "I'll just push this little red button and destroy the Decepticons!"

The teenage Autobot presses an iron finger on the Top Security button. A second later he presses his own panic button. Sirens are going off! Lights are flashing!

"Yikes!" Hot Rod yells.

"Run!" screams Bumblebee.

But it's too late. Iron bars clamp down over the doors of the room. On the monitors, the eyes of Galvatron focus on his prisoners.

"Fools!" the Decepticon leader sneers. "You fell into my trap. Now you can help me conquer the Autobots. Together, we will appear on television, and I will declare you my hostages. Ultra Magnus will do whatever I say to save you!"

Hot Rod covers his face in shame. He fell for the simple Decepticon trap. And now there are two more Autobots to rescue!

THE END

Hot Rod and Bumblebee slip out of Metroplex. The young Autobot wears a silver backpack. Inside are sophisticated new laser weapons just developed by Perceptor.

The duo transforms and speeds off to where Bumblebee sighted Astrotrain the night before. They wind south around tall trees and over hilly terrain to the deserted valley south of the Autobot city. Hot Rod zooms ahead and then spins on two wheels while Bumblebee catches up.

"Hey, do you hear that?" Hot Rod suddenly asks. The two Autobots cut their motors and sit silently in the midst of the towering pine trees. Around them, they hear the whisper of the branches swaying in the wind. But from a distance they can hear the mechanical sounds of robots.

Bumblebee blinks his headlights twice—their code to transform.

In their robot shape, Hot Rod and Bumblebee creep through the forest toward the noise. They reach an opening and gaze down at the valley below.

"Astrotrain!" Hot Rod exclaims.

The Decepticon space station sits in the valley. And all around it, like killer ants, swarm the Autobots' enemies!

. . . .

Turn to page 14.

While Ultra Magnus is busy giving orders, Powerglide and Swoop get ready for takeoff from the shuttle. "You're in charge of firepower," Powerglide says, "but remember, I do the fancy stuff."

Swoop flaps his delicate but powerful wings and gives Powerglide a goofy grin. Then, in unison, the two Autobots zoom off into space.

Halfway to Cyclonus, Powerglide turns on his side and veers right, heading straight into the transmissions being beamed to Earth by the Decepticon. Swoop, meanwhile, flies toward the back of the evil air warrior.

"This is it," Powerglide whispers to himself. He guns his engines to five hundred miles per hour and streaks across Cyclonus's view. An instant later a stutter of firepower spits from the huge Decepticon's artillery guns.

Powerglide loops up. He zigs left. He zags right. He drops straight down. And still Cyclonus hurls the unleashed fury of his weapons at the Autobot acrobat.

Powerglide is getting tired, but he knows he can't lose the enemy's attention for a second!

Watch out, Powerglide! That one was a little too close!

Turn to page 53.

The two Autobots scramble back to their feet and run to look out of Astrotrain's hatch.

"Dy-na-mite!" Hot Rod exclaims, gazing in amazement at the enemy ship.

Cyclonus drifts through space, a hole ripped through his side. In the far distance the Autobot space shuttle hovers cautiously. Meanwhile, inside Astrotrain, Decepticon voices are screeching in panic.

"Mission accomplished!" Hot Rod says proudly.

"I don't know about you," Bumblebee whispers, "but I'm hiding out for the rest of this trip. We'll find a way to escape when it docks."

The two Autobots climb into a big storage trunk filled with Laserbeak's dirty tricks—plastic spiders, rubber mice, and vampire fangs.

"Creepy," says Bumblebee, "but cozy."

"This should teach the Decepticons a lesson," Hot Rod adds with a grin. "Never pick up hitchhikers!"

THE END

A long moan comes from behind a rock in the crater. Hot Rod and Blurr rush to see who's there.

"Beachcomber!" Blurr exclaims. "What did they do to you?"

The Autobot geologist is tied up with explosive wire that is activated by the hot sun. His friends free him from the Decepticon device just before the wires blow up!

"They broke the code!" Beachcomber gasps.

"The ancient formula!" Hot Rod exclaims. "Do they know where it is?"

Beachcomber nods his head weakly.

"They flew . . . to raise the sunken ship . . . two hours ago," he murmurs before passing out.

Hot Rod and Blurr stare at each other in horror.

"Now we're sunk!" says Hot Rod.

Are you getting that sinking feeling? You goofed! Now the Decepticons will have the power booster. And that means ten times more of everything. Ten times more terror! Ten times more trouble!

THE END

In a few minutes two more Decepticons exit from the Space Gear room. One has the pants legs of his space suit rolled up. The other carries a silver backpack.

"I feel like I'm ready to trick-or-treat," Hot Rod complains.

"Quiet!" hisses Bumblebee.

Starscream and Thrust round a corner and advance toward the two Autobots. Their eyes seem to be boring holes through the silver space suits.

Will the disguises deceive the Decepticons? Or will the final countdown begin for Hot Rod and Bumblebee?

Turn to page 70.

"Forget it," says Bumblebee. "I think I just re-membered the code. I'll punch it in right now."

"No, I'll press the destruct button," Hot Rod in-sists.

Another argument! It's a good thing these guys have you around as a referee. This decision seems pretty simple—or is it?

Bumblebee can punch in a special code that will make the computer's bits and bytes go berserk. But does he really remember the right numbers?

Hot Rod doesn't know if the destruct button will really work. But all it takes is a little push to find out.

To punch in the computer code, turn to page 56.
To press the destruct button, turn to page 44.

"Bumblebee, I have a plan," the young Autobot whispers in his friend's ear. "Let's track down Astrotrain. I bet it's involved in the Decepticon space plot! We can take along the new laser-ignited explosives Perceptor just developed. Who knows, maybe we can do more than Ultra Magnus in his space shuttle!"

Just then Ratchet reports that the Autobot space shuttle is ready for blast-off. Ultra Magnus and the five other Autobots troop out to begin their flight into Earth orbit. Hot Rod and Bumblebee exchange excited grins.

You must make a choice. Do you want to go along with Hot Rod and Bumblebee? Their mission is daring and risky, but they could sabotage the Earth operations of the Decepticon space plot. Or do you want to go with Ultra Magnus and his team into space? They are flying into the unknown, but they have the power of the Autobot space shuttle with them.

Either way you go, it should be a blast!

. . . .

To follow Hot Rod and Bumblebee, turn to page 45.
To take off with Ultra Magnus in the shuttle, turn to page 18.

Swoop has reached the back of Cyclonus. He watches Powerglide dart across space, dodging a hailstorm of artillery. The Dinobot knows he hasn't a moment to lose. He readies his air-to-air missile launchers. Each one fires a charge equal to five thousand pounds of TNT!

"Cyclonus," says Swoop. "Swoop smash!"

The Dinobot unleashes a barrage of missiles at Cyclonus. A volley of destruction hits the Decepticon—its transmitters are blasted to smithereens!

"Decepticons get static now!" the Dinobot says with a big chuckle.

Swoop turns tail and flies back toward the Autobot space shuttle. Powerglide spins through the air to meet him, flashing his friend a victory sign.

Together again, they glance back at the blasted Cyclonus. The Decepticon is still trying to figure out what hit him!

Good decision making. The Autobots have triumphed. Earth is rescued from the reign of the Decepticons. And Bumblebee's TV set starts working again, just in time for his favorite show!

THE END

Following Galvatron's orders, a full force of Constructicons sink pilings into the ocean floor around the *Seville*. Working together as Devastator, they engineer the operation of lifting the ship.

Soon the Spanish galleon is raised from the water and deposited on the sandy beach.

In a cave just above the beach, Springer, Seaspray, and Topspin watch the enemy's every move.

"We must act *now!*" Springer says. Together the Autobots devise a strategy to steal the cybertite sphere right from under the Decepticons' noses. The two sea-assault robots will use diversionary tactics while Springer rescues the sphere.

Meanwhile, in another cave, Brawn, Grapple, and Ironhide plot a more forceful strategy. The "old heavies" of the Autobots want to hoist up the entire ship. They plan to use heavy artillery to defend it while a "lightweight" Autobot searches the hold for the sphere.

You're on the edge of a cliff with this decision. Which path will you choose?

. . . .

To go with Springer, turn to page 30.

To go with Brawn, Ironhide, and Grapple, turn to page 41.

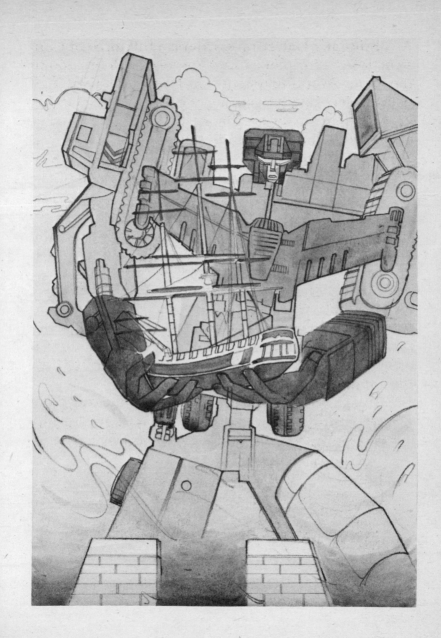

"Listen, kid," says Bumblebee, "I did a lot of homework in Advanced Espionage . . . and it's not going to go to waste! I'm punching in that code!"

"Okay, okay," Hot Rod mutters.

The little Autobot stands on his tippy-toes to reach the computer keyboard. He punches in a ten-digit code. Then he presses the Enter button.

The Autobots stare at the monitors on the walls around them. One shows Astrotrain spinning wildly out of control in space. Another shows Cyclonus, Galvatron's spaceship, completely immobilized. All the others show Galvatron's face turning purple with rage. Finally, he is totally blotted out by gray static.

"The Galvatron Horror Show is off the air," says Hot Rod. "By popular demand!"

"Let's get out of here!" shouts Bumblebee.

The two Autobots run for the exit. As soon as they're outside, they transform and take off in the direction of home.

The sky above the valley is lit by a fireworks display of orange, red, and blue explosions. One by one, the Decepticon computers blow themselves up!

For the Decepticons, it's definitely . . .

THE END

"The *Seville* never made it back to Spain," Springer explains. "It sank off the coast of California—and it's still there . . . with the cybertite sphere!"

"If the Decepticons break your code, they will know everything," Kup murmurs.

"They were heading for the meteor crater," Blurr interrupts. "IsawthemIsawthemIsawthemIsawthem!"

"If they haven't broken Springer's code," Ultra Magnus says, "they'll still be digging in the crater. But if they have broken the code, they'll find the wreck!"

"Let's go to the crater!" Springer cries. "We'll get back the message and destroy it before the Decepticons break the code."

"No, we may be too late for that," Kup insists. "We've got to head for the coast right away. The Autobots must raise the *Seville*—before the Decepticons do!"

You're at the command post again. You have two strategies to choose from. Which one of them is best?

. . . .

If you want the Autobots to go to the meteor crater, turn to page 65.

If you want them to speed to the California coast, turn to page 38.

Bumblebee sees his young friend standing alone. He walks over to join him.

"Guess we're stuck here," he says cheerily. "We'll hold down the fort."

"We're stuck all right," Hot Rod grumbles. "If only I could do something. I want to blast those Decepticons out of space!"

"Well, maybe there is something we can do," says Bumblebee. "I saw Astrotrain last night. It was hovering over a valley just south of here, as if it were on a spy mission. I figured it was one of the usual Decepticon transports . . . but now I wonder if this ties into their space plot."

Hot Rod's motor begins to hum with excitement. He's wondering what Astrotrain was doing too. Maybe, just maybe, he can be a hero yet! If Astrotrain is still stationed in the nearby valley, he could go there. And sabotage the Decepticon space plot!

Turn to page 52.

"Pull Cosmos aboard before Cyclonus sees us," Ultra Magnus orders. "Hurry!"

Jazz maneuvers the shuttle alongside the injured Autobot. He opens a huge hatch on the side of the vehicle. Powerglide and Mirage shoot out magnetic cables to latch on to the satellite. Soon Cosmos is safely inside the hold of the shuttle.

"I detect weak life signs," Mirage reports as he examines Cosmos. "But we need Ratchet to get him back in working order again."

"Report to control deck, report to control deck," the voice of Ultra Magnus booms over the intercom. The Autobots leave Cosmos and hurry to join their commander.

Turn to page 20.

On the cliff, Grapple frantically calls for Ratchet. His crane has had another breakdown! The Autobot mechanic goes to work, counting every second as the Decepticons draw nearer.

Finally Grapple is back in working order. He cranks up his steel cable, foot by foot, until Bumblebee and the *Seville* break through the surface of the water.

Hot Rod climbs out onto the long arm of Grapple's crane. It's his job to slide down the cable and search the ship for the cybertite sphere.

But wait! What's that sound?

Turn to page 39.

"Eons ago," Kup continues, "the Autobots lived on the planet of Cybertron. Even then, we were caught in the web of war spun by the Decepticons. Life there, like here, was a constant struggle against evil. That struggle required power. . . ."

Kup pauses dramatically.

"Imagine a power booster that could increase your strength ten times. Imagine using it in our battle against the Decepticons!"

A rumble of voices sweeps across the room.

"A formula for such a power booster exists," Kup exclaims. "It is the ancient Autobot secret!"

"But where is it?" Mirage calls out.

"On Cybertron the formula was encased in a sphere of cybertite—the only known piece of that rare mineral," Kup answers. "But there was a huge explosion on the planet, and the sphere was blown into space. We thought the formula was lost forever . . . until . . ."

A hush of silence falls over the room.

. . . .

Keep quiet and turn to page 6.

"Our fate is in your hands," Ultra Magnus tells Seaspray. "You must search the *Seville,* find the cybertite sphere, and bring it back to us—before the Decepticons arrive!"

The seagoing Autobot gulps. If he succeeds, he will go down in Autobot history. If he fails, they will all go down in Decepticon firepower.

The robot transforms into a naval defense vessel and speeds out over the ocean. Sighting the sunken ship below him, he switches back into his robot form—and dives.

Down, down, down to the floor of the ocean he goes. The *Seville* sits like a ghostly galleon amidst the seaweed and darting fish. Seaspray swims into its hold and begins his search.

In the captain's quarters he finds a rotting leather pouch. As he picks it up, a glowing green ball falls out. The cybertite sphere!

Seaspray grabs the ball and does an underwater somersault. His mission is a success! He swims out of the hold and—wait . . . what's that?

A shark!

Turn to page 9.

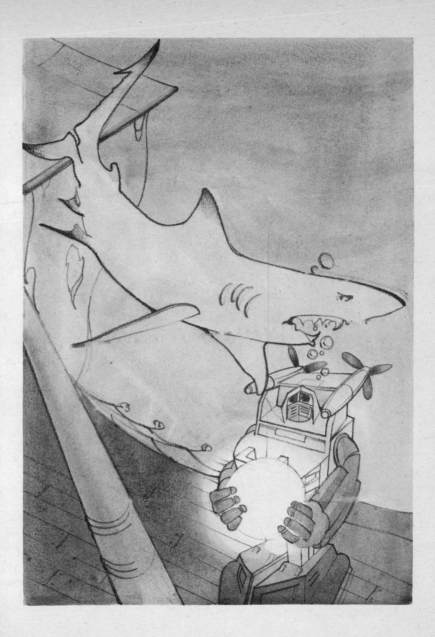

Astrotrain blasts off into space, leaving a cloud of thick smoke on the ground.

"Now's the time to make our move," Bumblebee whispers.

The Autobots dart through the gray cloud of exhaust toward the Decepticon complex. Hot Rod pulls a door open and they slip inside. Immediately the two take cover behind a bank of computers.

Soon the roar of Decepticon clapping shakes the building.

"Terrific takeoff!" one voice yells.

"Death to the Autobots!" adds another.

"Decepticons, rah! rah! rah!" screams a third.

Bumblebee and Hot Rod look at each other and roll their eyes. But a second later their attention is riveted to a TV monitor above them. The face of Galvatron smirks across the screen.

"Earthlings and Autobots!" he booms out, "this is your master speaking. Bow before your TV sets in my honor!"

Hey, don't bow! Just turn to page 66.

Hot Rod is the first to hear your decision to go to the meteor crater. He speeds ahead of the others, eager to impress Ultra Magnus.

The teenage Autobot raises a cloud of dust behind him as his wheels tear across the bare, parched land. As he nears the crater, he searches the sky for Decepticon planes. But the only thing he sees is the sun, burning like an orange ball of flame.

Suddenly a voice at his side surprises him.

"Race you to the crater, kid," Blurr challenges.

Hot Rod shifts into his highest gear. He strains his engine to accelerate. But Blurr is already out of sight!

Ten minutes later Hot Rod screeches to a stop at the edge of the crater.

"What took you so long, kid?" Blurr asks.

"Where are the Decepticons?" Hot Rod demands.

In front of them the crater stands like a huge, empty bowl.

If the Decepticons aren't here . . . where are they?

· ·

Turn to page 49.

"Who does he think he is?" Hot Rod mutters.

"Now's our time to move—while everybody is bowing to Galvatron," says Bumblebee. "The main computer room is over there. Let's sneak in."

Hot Rod nods in agreement. The two Autobots flash across the control center, unseen by the enemy. They slip into a room lined with hardware and monitors. Bumblebee begins to study the Decepticon system.

"The code!" he exclaims in frustration, staring at the keyboards. "What is that code?"

"What're you talking about?" asks Hot Rod.

"A code I learned in Advanced Espionage," Bumblebee explains. "It can scramble any Decepticon computer program. It's just that . . . I can't remember the last number!"

"Hey, wait a minute," says Hot Rod. "Look at that button on the wall!"

The two Autobots stare at a small, red button surrounded by four big black words—TOP SECURITY/ DESTRUCT SYSTEM!

"All we have to do is push that button," Hot Rod exclaims, "and we'll destroy the Decepticons!"

. . . .

Very interesting! Turn to page 51.

"Grapple, Bumblebee, Hot Rod . . . on the double!" Ultra Magnus orders.

The three Autobots speed up to their leader, who describes the difficult task facing them.

Grapple immediately transforms into a powerful crane. "Jump on," he tells Bumblebee.

The small robot hops onto the grappling hook at the end of the crane. Then Grapple swings his long arms out over the ocean.

"Okay, lower the boom!" Bumblebee shouts when he spies the sunken ship below.

Grapple spins out the steel cable that is attached to his hook. Slowly Bumblebee descends into the water. He rides Grapple's cable down through the ocean until it comes to rest on the sunken *Seville*. Bumblebee quickly secures the hook around the ship's mast and gives three quick tugs on the cable—his signal to Grapple to pull up.

Nothing happens.

Bumblebee gives three more tugs on the cable.

Still nothing happens.

Something had better happen soon!

Turn to page 60.

Hot Rod is going to try the military controls. "I don't care what happens to me!" he says. "I can't let Ultra Magnus fly into this trap!" The teenage Autobot marches straight toward Astrotrain's military command post.

Bumblebee trails nervously behind. "Act like you know what you're doing," the mini-car whispers as they approach the Decepticon guards. The disguised Autobots walk right past them into a room filled with computer hardware.

Hot Rod and Bumblebee go directly to a large monitor. It is tracking the positions in space of Astrotrain, Cyclonus, and the Autobot space shuttle. His eyes drop to the keyboard below it.

"I think I've got it," whispers Hot Rod. "I know how to deactivate Cyclonus!"

A tingle of fear is beginning to creep up Bumblebee's back. Something is wrong—very wrong—his instincts tell him. He whirls around.

Standing in the doorway is Scourge—the Decepticon scanner no Autobot can hide from . . . anywhere!

"Do it now!" Bumblebee commands Hot Rod. "Now!"

. . . .
Turn to page 17.

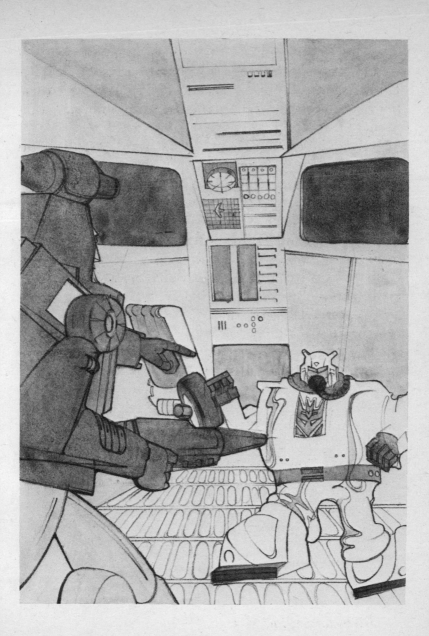

"Whew!" Hot Rod whispers as Starscream and Thrust pass by.

The two Autobots continue their inspection of Astrotrain.

"It's pretty risky wandering around like this," says Bumblebee. "We should find a hiding place and use those weapons!"

Just then the small Autobot looks out one of Astrotrain's side windows.

"Hot Rod, look!" he exclaims. "It's Cyclonus!"

The giant space warrior hovers in the black sky like a watchful spider.

"That's not all," adds Hot Rod, pointing to the right. "There's the Autobot space shuttle . . . and it's flying right into a Decepticon trap!"

Turn to page 19.

"Get the ship off the bottom!" Ultra Magnus yells, adding some unflattering words about Dinobots under his breath.

Sludge dives under the surface, splashing up a wave that reaches the top of the cliff. As the drenched Autobots shake the water out of their eyes, they see the Dinobot resurface . . . the cable clenched between his teeth and trailing from it, the *Seville*!

With one great heave Sludge drags the *Seville* to the top of the cliff. The Dinobots step back as he nudges it onto its side and tons of water spill out.

Hot Rod is ready. The second the flood subsides, the young robot goes to work. He jumps down the hatch into the hold of the ship and tears open every trunk and hiding place he sees. At last he finds the cybertite sphere!

Hot Rod runs up on deck with the glowing sphere held above his head.

Everyone on the cliff erupts into cheering. But Ultra Magnus booms out over their voices.

"Autobot alert! Autobot alert!"

The robots look into the eastern sky. Decepticon planes are advancing in a horde!

Turn to page 10.

Clenching the sphere in his hands, Springer climbs up onto the deck of the *Seville*. Then, with a powerful leap, he springs off the ship, high into the air, and lands on top of the cliff.

"Springer's got it!" the concealed Autobots cheer.

Out on the ocean, Seaspray and Topspin see the shining sphere in their friend's hands. They speed away from the Decepticons, leaving a trail of foam and dizzy fish.

Springer knows what to do next—get back to the Autobot city, pronto!

The powerful robot leaps from cliff to cliff, soaring above the deep chasms between the rocks. The rest of the Autobots hurry behind him, blasting away at the Decepticons.

Hours later Springer places the cybertite sphere in a secret vault in Metroplex. Perceptor has already read the formula it holds. He is in his lab, mixing up the ancient power booster.

Decepticons, beware! The balance of power has tipped. The forces of good are stronger than ever!

THE END